The Suitable Partner

OrangeBooks Publication

1st Floor, Rajhans Arcade, Mall Road, Kohka, Bhilai, Chhattisgarh 490020

Website: **www.orangebooks.in**

© **Copyright, 2024, Author**

All rights reserved. No part of this book may be reproduced, stored in a retrieval system, or transmitted, in any form by any means, electronic, mechanical, magnetic, optical, chemical, manual, photocopying, recording, or otherwise, without the prior written consent of its writer.

First Edition, 2024
ISBN: 978-93-6554-043-7

The Suitable Partner

The Life Beyond Imagination

Orange Books Publication
www.orangebooks.in

The Suitable Partner
(The Life Beyond Imagination)

When Reality hits, the imaginary world falls but the outcome may be even better.

Introduction

Let me introduce you to Rahul's family and their situation. Rahul comes from a middle-class family in Jaipur. His father, Karan, is an employee at a bank, while his mother, Neeta, is a homemaker and teaches Math, Science, and English to students. Rahul excels in both academics and sports. He has a passion for music and is enthusiastic about dance. He has a younger sister named Disha, who is in the 9th grade, while Rahul is in the 11th grade.

Situation 1 (Rahul and his friends Mohit, Vinay, Raj, and Abhishek participate in the Youth fest in their city).

Rahul: When are they going to start the fest, Mohit?

Mohit: I think in 15 minutes

(Rahul gives a frustrated look, and meanwhile, the dance starts)

Mohit: Hey Rahul, I believe it started.

(Rahul sits beside Mohit hesitatingly)

Rahul gets mesmerized by a girl's Kathak performance and is attracted by her beauty. He tries to find her in the school but learns that she is only in the 7th grade.

He participates in the sports event but gets a 3rd place as his mind deviates.

Rahul's father: What's wrong with you, Rahul? Where were you? How come third place this time?

Rahul: Sorry, dad. I couldn't concentrate this time.

Rahul's father: This is the first time, child, that you have been placed 3rd. I am concerned about you.

Rahul's mother (to her husband): "It's alright, Karan. He must be feeling stressed about his studies since he's in 11th grade now," she says, encouraging Rahul to relax. However, Rahul couldn't stop thinking about the girl. After a while, his mother calls him and his sister, Disha, for dinner. They all eat together before heading off to bed.

The Next morning

Mohit: Hey Rahul, are you there? (Knocking at the door at Rahul's place)

Rahul's mother: Hello, beta. How are you? Come inside and have breakfast with us.

Mohit: Thank you, aunty. I had it. Where is Rahul? He seemed upset yesterday.

Rahul's mother: But do you have any idea? He also got a 3rd place this time.

Mohit: Aunty, that dance. hmmm

(Mohit suddenly shuts his mouth)

Rahul's mother: (suspecting the secret) Are you people hiding anything from us?

Mohit: No, no, auntie, it's nothing. I was just about to say that he loves to dance but didn't get a chance to participate this time.

(Rahul's mother whispered to herself, "I don't understand these boys, especially as this generation gets crazier.")

Rahul's mother: Go and meet your friend. He is still in bed. Wake him up.

(Mohit goes to Rahul's bedroom to wake him up)

Rahul is still dreaming about the girl and him doing salsa.

Mohit: Hey, Rahul. (Doesn't get up) Hey Rahul... (still dreaming) (Mohit shakes him like anything)

Rahul: (Wonders) Why does Mohit call him while dancing with his dream girl!!

Rahul awoke suddenly from a deep sleep.

Rahul: Hey, Mohit, you broke my dream (furiously). It was a wonderful dream with my dream girl. I was dancing with her. How come you are here?

Mohit: Can't you get over this stupid thing? I know you lost to Mahaveer International School (the one who got first in the running) because of this obsession. It is just a crush, buddy. Forget it; besides, we are still in 11th grade, and she is just a kid. The 12th grade is crucial for us. Don't you want to get into IITs or NITs? Think about it.

Rahul suddenly realizes that he should study hard to get into the top institutes and shifts his focus to learning.

After 1 year

Rahul and Mohit cleared IIT JEE and entered IIT Bombay.

Rahul is in his first year and very enthusiastic about his studies. His first year runs well. Here comes the second year and the twist in his life.

Alisha enters IIT Bombay as his immediate junior.

Let us know Alisha's background. Alisha is a modern girl from a wealthy family. She has an attitude, and her father, Mr. Shailesh Aggarwal, is a businessman. He has a chain of hotels worldwide. They have a spacious bungalow and servant quarters with more than 20 servants assigned to different tasks. She has a very different approach to life. She gets everything in place as and when required.

She has a lavish lifestyle and is the only daughter of Mr. Shailesh Aggarwal and Mrs. Shashikala Aggarwal. Her mother, Shashikala, is a mathematics professor at IIT Bombay. Unlike her husband and daughter, Shashikala is a straightforward woman. She doesn't like her daughter's attitude towards life. But Alisha is more inclined towards a luxurious life.

Shashikala always shows her daughter the other side of life. Unfortunately, it doesn't work, and Mr. Aggarwal scolds her.

If God has blessed her with this life, why must she look at the other side? This is what Alisha thinks.

On the first day of her college

In her brand-new Audi A7 Sport, Alisha arrives at the college. She gets out of the car in her modern attire: pointed heels, jeans, and a black top. All eyes in college are on her, including the girls.

All the boys want to introduce themselves to her. She is self-obsessed. Meanwhile, Rahul and Mohit arrive to see the new girl, and both get captivated by her beauty. Seniors, stop ragging and start being innocent with her.

Mohit: Hey Rahul, can I make her fall in love with me? She looks rich, man. Look at her brand-new Audi. Look at her height, personality, and color. I can settle down without any effort.

Rahul: (Gives a sarcastic smile.) Mohit bhai, look at your face, man. You need a lot more effort to grab her attention. Love is far beyond.

Mohit: So, do you think you can grab her attention? If you think you are handsome as compared to me.

Rahul: I don't give a damn about such girls, Mohit (But he is genuinely enamored by her and pretending to avoid her.)

Mohit pays a little attention to Alisha. But Rahul ignores her and walks away.

Mohit: Hey Rahul, how could you ignore such a beautiful girl?

(Rahul starts the bike and heads back to the hostel.)

Rahul: Now, see the magic.

Mohit: You are crazy, man. How could you?

When everyone surrounds Alisha, she notices that Rahul is not looking at her.

Rahul (To his mother on call): Hey, Mom, how are you doing?

Rahul's mother: I am fine. How are you, and how is your sophomore year going?

Rahul: Mom, I am fine. Everything is running well. I also need to tell you something.

Rahul's mother: Do you have a girlfriend? Hey, just let me know. (suspiciously)

Rahul: Mom, cool down. It's definitely about a girl, but it's not about a girlfriend.

Rahul's mother: Don't keep me waiting. Tell me.

Rahul: It's about the girl who joined today. She is in her first year and is beautiful. She came in an Audi A7 sports mom.

Rahul's mother: Son, I do not want to interfere in your life. First, you need to settle down, and then you can attract any girl, dear. This is just a suggestion; I am not against you.

Rahul: Hey mom, I just saw her today. I don't know her either. Just leave her. How are you all doing?

Rahul's mother: We are all doing fine beta. Take care. See you.

Rahul: Bye mom. See you.

The next day morning in the college:

Alisha enters the college campus, and everybody starts staring at her. She is wearing a blue frock. Rahul once again ignores her and goes to his classroom. Alisha constantly observes Rahul and his indifference.

All the seniors are planning Fresher's Day for the new batch and finally, they keep it a week later.

Alisha and her friends are preparing for an introductory program that includes speeches, dance performances, singing, painting, and many other activities. The seniors are organizing the event, and Rahul serves as the anchor. His friends, including Mohit, are assisting him in scheduling everything properly.

Rahul and Mohit had met the juniors that week to discuss their activities. In this situation, Rahul again ignores Alisha and sends Mohit to inquire about them. Alisha wonders about this and talks to one of her friends.

Alisha: Hey, Sania, what do you think about this guy?

Sania: Who? Mohit. He is good, but I love Rahul. He is so handsome. (She blushes.)

Alisha: Forget about Mohit; I'm talking about Rahul. Don't you think he is crazy? While the whole college is after me, this guy has so much attitude—he's not even looking at me.

Sania: He might like me, Alisha. I should give it a try on him.

Alisha: I don't believe he is your type. Look at you. Try Mohit; it might work.

Sania: I have to leave (furiously). You try on Mohit.

Sania murmurs to herself (What does she think of herself and leaves)

Alisha: Get lost.

While Alisha practices her dance and singing, Rahul quietly watches her, pretending to ignore her. A week passes, and finally, Fresher's Day arrives.

Alisha is all set to impress the audience, ready to perform on stage. The boys eagerly await her performance, while the girls, feeling jealous, try to prove that they are better than Alisha.

On the Freshers Day

Rahul is hosting the program and is all set to start it.

Rahul: Respected teachers, fellow students, and dear juniors, I welcome you all to the Freshers' Gathering. Congratulations to all the juniors for being accepted into such a prestigious institute. I won't take much of your time with speeches, so let's begin the program.

First, I would like to introduce you to our college. (He introduced it.)

Next, I would like to introduce you to our lecturers.

Mohit introduces all the lecturers.

Rahul: Now, it is the time for our junior's introduction. (He calls them one by one to introduce themselves.)

Other girls like Sania, Maheshwari, Neeta, and Rashmi are as beautiful as Alisha, but boys still find Alisha different. Now, everyone introduces themselves, and then it's Alisha's turn.

As Alisha steps on the stage, Rahul cannot take his eyes off her (but still, he pretends not to like her), and all the other boys are deeply smitten by her beauty. She introduces herself and performs a small dance. Many other students, like Sania, Maheshwari, Neeta, and Rashmi, also perform their dances.

On the other hand, Mohit is also captivated by Alisha's beauty and compliments her in front of Sania. Now……

Mohit: Oh, my gosh! God must have devoted much of his time creating this beauty. (Looking towards Alisha when Alisha waves him back.)

Rahul: That is true. But how come God did not invest any of his time in creating you? I don't understand. (All the others laugh along with Rahul, and Rahul goes to the library.)

Sania, who is listening to all this, along with her friends speaks-

Sania: Outer beauty fades, dear Mohit, but inner beauty is what truly matters. Do you take the time to understand a person's heart? There are many other qualities to discover beyond just external appearances. (Mohit looks at her for a while.)

Sania expresses this to Mohit because she feels jealous of Alisha.

Sania may not be conventionally beautiful, but she is a genuinely good person.

The Next morning
Mohit is silent

Rahul: What's wrong with you? You're not even answering my calls.

Mohit doesn't talk

Rahul: I'll slap you now. If you don't answer.

Mohit comes to the talking terms

Mohit: Rahul, I feel like I am being swept away.

Rahul: Shall we consult a psychiatrist?

Mohit: Hey, no. I think I like somebody.

Rahul: Hey, I know that. Go and propose to her, man. But she might reject you because everyone likes her. She is the most beautiful girl in the college.

Mohit: Why would she reject me?

Rahul: Because she is beautiful.

Mohit: You never said this before. Anyway, I am not that bad.

Rahul: Then let us make an attempt and see if she talks to you.

Mohit: Really? Then let's talk to her.

Rahul: Look there she is.

Mohit: Where?

Rahul: Right in front of that café.

Mohit: Where man?

Rahul: I think you have also gone blind in her love.

Mohit: No. Sania is not there.

Rahul: Are you talking about Sania?

Mohit: Yes. Of course. I thought you understood me.

Rahul: Are you serious Mohit? Sania? Not Alisha, right? Yesterday, you complimented her, and I thought so.

Mohit: Yes, it is Sania not Alisha. Alisha is good but not my type.

Rahul: Ok. Look, she is coming. Talk to her.

Mohit: Hi Sania.

Sania: Hi Mohit. How come here?

Mohit: I want to understand people. Some people are good human beings, and don't need outlooks. Their talks and nature determine them. I want to know you.

Sania smiles and goes. Mohit follows her.

Mohit: Can we have a cup of coffee?

Sania: OK. Let us have it in the break.

Mohit and Sania spend time together in the café and got along.

At night
Rahul asks Mohit about the coffee date with Sania.

Rahul: How was the coffee date with Sania today?

Mohit: It was fantastic, Rahul. She is so humble and down to earth, and she is adorable. I like her.

Rahul: Is she better than Alisha?

Mohit: I know Alisha has grabbed your attention, but you are pretending to avoid her. Yes, I had a crush on Alisha in the beginning, but I don't know how I developed feelings for Sania in two days.

Rahul: Ok. If you are damn serious about her then I am happy for you, my friend. All the best.

Mohit: Thank you, Rahul, my friend. Hope I'll see you and Alisha together soon.

Rahul: Hmm. Let's see.

They go to sleep.

The Next morning

Mohit and Sania start their relationship and Rahul feels lonely. Meanwhile, Alisha sees that Rahul doesn't want to become an obstacle between Mohit and Sania and stays apart leaving them alone. Alisha keeps watching him.

He doesn't express his feelings to Alisha as well. And a week passes by. One fine day, Alisha and her friends are hanging out after their classes, and suddenly, she collapses due to sunstroke. Her friends become dumbstruck, and Sania calls Mohit, and Mohit informs Rahul.

Rahul immediately asks for their location and starts his bike. He sees her condition and immediately admits her to the nearby hospital. After some time, she comes to consciousness and thanks her friends. Maheshwari and

Sania say that she should thank Rahul who immediately admitted her to the hospital.

Rahul comes to the hospital and asks about her well-being. She thanks him and asks her friends to vacate the room for some time, as she needs to talk to Rahul personally.

Alisha: Can we talk for a while Rahul?

Rahul: Yes, of course, tell me.

Alisha: I want to ask you something.

Rahul: Ya, please.

Alisha: On the first day of my college, everyone was staring at me except you. I know you watched but still avoided me. Don't you like me? At least as friends? Everyone speaks to me well. You never did. But you secretly watch me, why?

Rahul: Looks at the other side for some time (Doesn't know what to say and how to react) and says I don't know it is just that I never speak to girls. (Starts going out.)

Alisha: Stop Rahul. She gets up, holds his hand, and asks if he likes her.

Rahul: Yes (Spontaneously).

They hug each other.

All the friends from outside the room (Sania, Maheshwari, Rashmi, Nisha, and others) come inside and surround them, singing "Yeh toh hona hi tha." And dance.

Alisha: Why did you come inside? I asked you to vacate and leave us alone for some time, no?

Maheshwari: Don't worry, we won't come with you on your first night.

Rashmi: Bear with us for some time. After some time, you will escape like anything.

Everyone laughs.

Sania: Hey all, let us celebrate the beginning of your relationship with all our friends.

Rahul: Let us call the whole group and enjoy.

Rahul calls Mohit

Rahul: Hey Mohit, where are you?

Mohit: I am in the college campus with our group. How is Alisha now?

Rahul: She is fine. I have some good news for you.

Mohit: What is that?

Rahul: Alisha and I are together.

Mohit: Means??

Rahul: Understand, man.

Mohit: Oh my God! Congratulation's man.

Rahul: Thank you. We all want to celebrate this new beginning. Can you please come to the Ajanta café? You, too, started a new relationship just a few days back, right?

Mohit: Ya. We don't want to become a weed between two loving flowers. You both spend some time alone.

Rahul: Don't be so grateful for me now. I know how you pull my legs. We would be spending time with each other for our whole life. Right now, I want to celebrate with all of you, and I won't listen to any of you. Just be there within 30 minutes.

Rahul cuts the call

All the friends gather at the Ajanta café and celebrate the new relationship.

Rahul: Hey, all cheers to the new beginning. (Holding a beer.)

Maltesh (to Alisha): Alisha Bhabhi, we did not want to create a hindrance between you both. Rahul called us.

Alisha (To Maltese): Don't call me Bhabhi in the first place. Call me Alisha. And it's okay; we are celebrating with friends; I don't mind.

Maltesh: Ok. Alisha ma. (In a namaste pose). Can we eat something now?

Alisha: Do I look like a mom?

Maltesh: No Grand ma. Just kidding.

Rahul: Ok. Ok, let us order some pizzas and pasta.

They eat, enjoy, drink, and go back to their respective homes.

At night

Rahul drops Alisha. They talk for some time and she goes.

Rahul and Alisha keep on talking on the phone all night and don't sleep.

Rahul (Calls Alisha): Hi Alisha

Alisha: Hi Rahul.

Rahul: Whats up?

Alisha: It's YOU, creating butterflies in my tummy.

Rahul: Oh my God it's too much. Can't digest this.

Alisha: Then what do you expect me to keep up with?

Rahul: I did not expect you to like me.

Alisha: Really!!

And the conversation goes on till the next morning.

The next morning

Rahul and Alisha arrive late to the campus. The gatekeeper did not let them enter the class, so they went on a ride and spent some time together.

On the other hand, Mohit and Sania continue with their relationship, and both the couple friends enjoy their college days.

One fine day (Rahul's mother calls him)

Neeta: Hi Rahul. How are you beta?

Rahul: I am fine, mom. How are you?

Neeta: I want to tell you something about Disha.

Rahul: Yes, mom. Tell me.

Neeta: Disha is not studying well. I think she is in a relationship.

Rahul: Did you talk to her?

Neeta: Yes, I did. But she is not talking to me appropriately.

Rahul: I'll talk to her then. That's okay, mom. I am coming to Jaipur and will talk to her in person.

Neeta: Ok.

Rahul has to travel to Jaipur and plans to take Alisha, Mohit, Sania, and Maltesh with him.

Rahul (to Alisha, Mohit, Maltesh, and Sania): Hey guys, I plan to visit my hometown. I would like you all to join with me.

They all agree and plan for the journey.

Rahul (to Alisha): If you don't mind, can you wear Indian outfits like kurtas or sarees when you meet my family?

Alisha: Why?

Rahul: Please try to understand, Alisha. Indian families expect that from a girl, at least during an introduction.

Alisha: I am a modern, independent girl who wants to live on my terms and conditions.

Rahul: I don't want to argue with you. Be the way you want.

Alisha: Please don't be angry. Did you tell your parents about us?

Rahul: No. I haven't. I will let them know at the right time.

Everyone travels to Jaipur with excitement.

At Rahul's residence!!!!!!

Rahul's mother welcomes everyone. Here, Alisha is in her modern attire. They rest for some time and visit different places in Jaipur.

Alisha observes the house and then.

Alisha: Is the house not too small for you all?

Rahul: It doesn't matter; we are happy. Alisha, I know that you belong to a rich family. But you should know how to lead a normal life.

At the dinner table

All the friends sit and chat. Rahul's mother serves them dinner.

Alisha (To Neeta): Aunty, don't you have servants to cook?

Neeta: No, Beta. I love cooking, and I do it myself. Do you have servants at your place?

Alisha: Yes, Aunty. We have many.

Neeta: Oh, you must be rich then.

Alisha: Nothing like that, aunty.

Neeta: Just kidding. Have your dinner.

Alisha doesn't like his house. She feels it is too small and they were not very rich too, but she pretends to like it.

At night!!!!!
Everyone sleeps, and Neeta talks to Rahul.

Neeta: Rahul, did you talk to Disha?

Rahul: No, mom, I'll talk to her now. Don't worry.

Rahul goes to talk to his sister Disha. Rahul knocks at Disha's door.

Rahul: Hi Dish. How are you?

Disha: I am OK, bro. How about you?

Rahul: How are your studies going on ? And look, here are some chocolates for you.

Disha: It is going well; bro. Thank you for the chocolates. How are you?

Suddenly, she gets a call from her boyfriend.

Disha: Bro, it's my friend's call. I need to talk. Can I talk to you later?

Rahul: Ya sure.

Rahul goes away.

Neeta calls him and speaks.

Neeta: Rahul, see her.

Rahul: Mom, I know. I'll do something about this. Don't worry.

Neeta: She is in her 12th grade. We should do something before it's too late.

Rahul: Don't worry, I'll handle this.

The next morning

Rahul follows Disha to see what is going on exactly in her life and where she was going. He continuously follows her along with Maltesh. Rahul and Maltesh find out that she is in a relationship with a fraud guy involved in human trafficking.

Rahul and Maltesh get his (Rohan's) number and call him. They approach him for a business deal and try to become friends. **Rahul:** Is this Rohan speaking?

Rohan: Yes, may I know who is speaking to me?

Rahul: It doesn't matter who we are. We have a business deal and want to meet you.

Rohan: What deal do you have?

Rahul: Can't talk on the phone. Let's meet.

Rohan: Ok.

They meet at the bar.

Rahul: Hey Rohan, let us have a drink.

Maltesh: Ya man, it's been a long time

Rohan: Ya sure.

They take a very small drink and force Rohan to drink more. After a while, Rohan starts blabbering things out.

Rahul: Hey Rohan, be frank, man. How do you manage to earn your livelihood?

Rohan: It's a secret (In a drunkard mode with each gulp.)

Rahul: Say it, my dear buddy, we all are brothers here.

Rohan doesn't spit everything in one go. But slowly starts.

Rohan: I make girls fall in love with me and mmm….

Rahul: And???

Rohan: And nothing.

Maltesh: If you tell the secret. We have a good deal for you.

Rohan: What deal?

Maltesh: Business deals with crores of profit.

Rohan: Really?

Maltesh: Ya.

Rohan: Ok.

Rohan spits out the secret.

Rohan (to Maltesh and Rahul): I am handsome. Am I?

Maltesh and Rahul: Yes, of course.

Rohan: I make teen girls fall in love with me and sell them. Simple. We have a big team in Mumbai.

Rahul (In a furious mode. He controls and comes back): So, how many girls have you sold till now?

Rohan: Maybe 100 or even more.

Rahul finds out from his contacts that Rohan at present has more than 25 girlfriends, and his sister Disha is one of them. He shows her picture to him.

Rahul: Do you recognize her?

Rohan: I think I know her. Yes, she is Disha.

Rahul: What are you going to do with her now?

Rohan: I am manipulating her. In 15 days, she will escape and elope with me to Bangalore, and from there, she will go to Mumbai. I am responsible until then.

Rahul: Ok. Let us go.

Rahul and Maltesh do not react and go home. But Maltesh records everything using a pen camera.

Rahul (to Disha): Disha, I need to show you something.

He shows her the video. Disha gets shattered and sits on a chair for a while. After a while, she starts crying heavily. She apologizes to Rahul.

Disha: I am sorry, bro. I was about to elope with him. I am sorry for whatever I did. I couldn't concentrate on my studies; I had lost all my senses as he manipulated me so well.

Rahul: How did you come into his contact?

Disha: Around six months ago, after the summer holidays, he used to stand in front of the school gate every day. Once, I suddenly fell from my bicycle, and he lifted me. He then repaired my bicycle and dropped me home. We exchanged numbers and started chatting, which led to further meeting each other and falling in love.

Rahul stops Neeta, who is about to slap her. Karan (her father) gets upset and goes to his bedroom. Rahul takes Disha outside to talk.

Rahul: The past is past. Nobody can change it. But Disha, you are small, and the world is dangerous. You should be careful. Falling in love is not bad, but with the wrong person, it can be disastrous. Please be careful. Concentrate on your studies.

Disha: Sorry bro, I won't commit this kind of a blunder again. Forgive me.

Rahul: From today onwards, you must share everything with either mom or dad or at least me. Promise?

Disha: Yes.

Rahul: Let us apologize to, dad and mom.

Disha: I am scared

Rahul: Don't be. They are our parents.

Disha apologizes to her parents and everything resolves smoothly.

Rahul and his friends go back to Mumbai for their studies.

Rahul and his friends enjoy their studies, college, and relationships.

One fine day at Alisha's residence

Alisha's mother, who knows everything about her, starts talking to her husband.

Shashikala: Shailesh, have you seen your daughter?

Shailesh: Why? What happened to her?

Shashikala: She is in a relationship with her senior, Rahul.

Shailesh: What?? (Enraged) And now you are letting me know this???

Shashikala: Rahul is not a bad guy Shailesh.

Shailesh: Oh! Now you decide everything by yourself without my consent? You could have taken care of this as you teach in the same institute. How can you be such an irresponsible, mother? I want her to get married into a prestigious family. And you spoiled it.

Shashikala: I don't have time to argue with you. Rahul is a good human being. But your daughter doesn't suit him. Better talk to her.

Shailesh: I don't understand.

Shashikala: You have spoiled her by giving her all the luxuries. (She walks away)

Shailesh doesn't talk.

Shailesh calls Alisha, who is in the campus.

Shailesh: Where are you?

Alisha: In the college campus, dad. Why?

Shailesh: Are you with Rahul, right?

Alisha: Dad, he is my friend.

Shailesh: We need to talk as soon as possible. (He cut the call).

Alisha tells Rahul that her father has come to know about their relationship.

Alisha: Rahul, dad knows everything about us, and I am afraid he will deny it.

Rahul: It's ok we will manage. Don't worry.

Alisha goes back home.

At Alisha's Residence

Alisha and her father talk

Shailesh: How was your day, Alisha?

Alisha: It was pretty good dad.

Shailesh: I need to talk.

Alisha: Ya sure. Tell me

Shailesh: I don't want to beat around the bush. So, are you in a relationship with Rahul?

Alisha: mmmmm (Hesitant)

Shailesh: Yes, or No?

Alisha: Yes.

Shailesh: I had vast expectations from you, and you broke them apart. I sent you to the coaching centre, and gave you beyond your expectations, but now that I see it, you are not worth it.

Shashikala: Rahul is not a bad guy Shailesh. He is a gem.

Shailesh: Stop, Shashi. (Infuriated). You spoiled her, not me. I do not want to talk to you.

Shashikala goes away.

Shailesh: What kind of family does Rahul belong to?

Alisha: I don't know.

Shailesh: So, without even knowing about him you fell in love. Great!!!

Alisha: How does it even matter?

Shailesh: It matters a lot. I wanted to give you to the wealthiest person and expand my business. One more thing is that you won't be able to adjust to the middle-class family, dear.

Alisha: Hey, dad, I understand, but please meet him once and decide.

Shailesh: Ok. Call him for a dinner tonight.

Alisha: Are you kidding?

Shailesh: I am serious.

Alisha: Thanks Dad.

Alisha calls him for dinner and he agrees.

At Alisha's Residence

Rahul arrives. Alisha introduces him to the family.

Shailesh: Hi Rahul, Welcome.

Shashikala: Please come inside.

Alisha: Thanks for coming.

They go inside the living room to chat.

Shailesh asks Shashikala to bring wine for both of them.

Shailesh starts the conversation.

Shailesh: So, young boy, how are you?

Rahul: I am good, sir; how about you?

Shailesh: I am good. Thank you. Getting into IITs is not that simple. Which coaching center did you join?

Rahul: I did not join any coaching center in the specification. However, my cousins shared some study materials and helped me clear this. My parents' blessings and my hard work helped me to get into the IIT.

Shailesh: Oh, that's great. Congratulations. I appreciate it.

Rahul: Thank you, sir.

Meanwhile, Shashikala arrives with two glasses of wine.

Shailesh: Did you see this house? The servants? The luxury here?

Rahul: Yes, I know you are rich and can afford everything.

Shailesh: Rahul, it's not about me being rich. Alisha has been raised in this kind of environment, and she cannot adjust to a middle-class family.

Rahul: Sir, anybody can become rich if they are determined. I am determined to do something great in life, and I am confident that I'll achieve it—maybe even better than you.

Shailesh: I like your spirit. Have the wine.

CHEERS!! They all drink wine.

Shailesh calls Alisha.

Shailesh: Alisha, I was angry with you. But now I can say that your choice is the best. Go ahead and enjoy.

Alisha: Thank you, dad, I didn't expect this from you.

Shailesh: He is as determined as I was during my struggling days. This determination helps us to reach our destination.

Alisha thanks her dad and goes with Rahul.

Shashikala: Did I not tell you that Rahul is a nice guy? You had simply blasted on me and now you accepted their relationship. I won't talk to you anymore.

Shailesh: Sorry Shashi!! I was scared about her future. Please forgive me.

Shashikala: It's ok. You are always the same.

Shailesh: Sorry again.

They both come to the talking terms.

Now, Rahul worries that his mother dislikes Alisha because he hasn't informed them about his relationship, and Alisha's impression is not great.

They complete their studies and all their friends get into various companies after their placement tests.

Rahul informs his family about his relationship .

Neeta: Rahul, Alisha is not suitable for our family.

Rahul: How can you say this, mom? I know she is a little different, but I love her. Eventually, everything will fall into place. Please give me some time.

Neeta: I am not against your love but she is a little stubborn. I am afraid if…….

Rahul: I will look into this mom. I'll change her bit by bit.

Sania, Mohit, Alisha, and Rahul are busy with their jobs and relationships. They go on trips, and time flies.

Rahul's family also approves of their relationship.

One day Alisha visits Rahul's place.

Rahul's mother asks Rahul and Alisha to visit the temple along with her. Rahul takes her to the temple and Alisha is wearing an Indian attire here. She is chatting on her phone and Panditji watches it multiple times. While taking prashadam the mobile falls and Panditji says-

Panditji: See child, this is not the way to do pooja. Give some respect to God. May God bless you.

Alisha: My parents never advised me anything, and now you want to teach me how to pray. Look, I belong to an affluent family. Don't you dare teach me?

Alisha creates a big scene and all of them gather in the temple and start gossiping about Neeta and her mannerless would-be daughter-in-law.

Neeta sends Rahul and Alisha back home and talks to Panditji.

Neeta: Panditji, I apologize to you on behalf of her. She belongs to a very rich family and my son loves her a lot. I couldn't resist. Please forgive her.

She falls to his feet.

Panditji: I may forgive you, and God also forgives, but looking at her tantrums, she will spoil your family. Take care, Neetaji.

Neeta: Thank you Panditji. I'll do something about this.

Neeta talks to Rahul about Alisha. But Rahul ensures that Alisha will eventually change over the period and everything will be sorted, as he is madly in love with her.

Rahul and Alisha and Sania and Mohit continue their relationship.

1-year passes, and one fine day, Alisha's Uncle (father's brother) and aunty arrive at their residence from Ahmedabad.

Shivraj (Uncle): Hey Shailesh and Shashi. How are you?

Shreedevi (Aunty): Hey, Shailesh, bro, and Shashi. How are you all? How is Alisha? I guess she is a big girl now.

Shailesh and Shashikala: We all are fine. Of course, sis. She is a big girl now. Please come inside. How are you all? How are Sahana and Sadhana?

Shreedevi: You all know Sadhana and Alisha are same age. And Sahana is working.

Shashikala: You could have brought them along with you Shree!!

Shivraj: Sadhana is on her way. She will arrive by evening.

Shashikala: I'll get some drinks for you.

(Shashikala gets some juice and wine for them)

Shailesh: It's been a long time bro. I am glad to see you both.

Shashikala: Yes absolutely.

Shivraj: Hey Shailesh you could have visited us in these 6 years. You didn't turn up.

Shailesh: No, bro. I am stressed out with my work, and I hardly talk to Shashi and Alisha.

Shivraj: I know you and thus decided to visit you once.

Shailesh: Thank you, bro. I am very glad to see you both.

Shivraj: Hey Alisha, my girl, how are you?

Alisha: I am keeping good. How are you?

Shreedevi: Look, Shiv. She is so tall and beautiful. She used to play a lot with Sadhana.

Shivraj: Ya I remember.

Meanwhile, Sadhana arrives, and everybody welcomes her. Sadhana and Alisha sit together and share their memories of college, friends, etc.

Alisha: Hey Sadhana, do you have a boyfriend?

Sadhana: It's complicated. But I think we are friends. I am not sure. (confused)

Alisha: You can share.

Sadhana: There is nothing to share. Okay, let me tell you. His name is Yuvraj, and he is an industrialist. He proposed to me, but I had borrowed some time.

Shashikala: Hey, don't you want to spend time with us?

Sadhana: Yes, aunty. Let's go. Let's talk later Alisha.

They go and start the dinner
On the dinner table

Shailesh: Hey bro, What about Sahana? Any marriage plans for her? I know these days girls prefer a career over marriage.

Shivraj: When she has planned everything, we don't need to take stress.

Shashikala: Means? Love marriage?

Shreedevi: Yes. This is one of the reasons we came to you. She is getting married, and it's a love marriage. The boy is in Canada. His father has a business empire. He works for a startup now, but later, he will take over all the businesses.

Shashikala (Astonished): Congratulations bro and Shree. We are so happy for you.

Shreedevi: Thank you, Shashi.

Alisha: Congratulations to Uncle, Aunty, and Sahana di.

Shivraj and Shreedevi: Thank you Beta.

Shashikala: When are you solemnizing the marriage? And how did she find him? I am so curious to know.

Shreedevi: The marriage is on 20th November. Well, Anurag is her childhood friend, and we dealt with his father in our business. One day after college, suddenly, she came to us and said she was in a relationship. We got scared, but after we got to know him and his family, we got relaxed.

Later, after 4 years of courtship, they are getting married.

Shailesh: Great to know that you know each other. Hearty congratulations once again.

Shashikala: Can you show me Anurag's picture?

Sadhana shows Sahana and Anurag's picture to Shailesh and Shashikala.

Shailesh: Wow! Handsome and tall guy you people are lucky.

Shashikala: Nice pair. They are made for each other.

Shivraj: He is well-mannered, handsome, and, more than anything, a good human being.

Shailesh: That is the most important thing in life.

Shashikala: If you both need anything we are here for you. Let us celebrate this marriage.

Shivraj: Thanks a lot, Shailesh, Shashi and Alisha.

Alisha: Where is Sahana sis now?

Shreedevi: She is working on a project, dear, and is deputed to Pune.

Alisha: Oh! That's great

They stay for a night and leave for Ahmedabad.

Everything goes well, and Alisha asks her parents' permission to invite her friends to Sahana's wedding along with Rahul. They agree. All the friends, along with Alisha and her parents, go to Ahmedabad. The celebration lasts for seven days, and all of them participate in the dance, Mehendi, Haldi, and Bachelor's party.

On the first day of the celebration, Alisha meets her would-be brother-in-law, Anurag Saxena, and introduces all her friends to him. She understands that his father has a big empire, and Anurag will carry it forward. Everyone is dumbfounded by the gifts, jewelry, and sarees given by Anurag's family.

Shashikala: Wow! Shree, this family is so fantastic. The arrangements, jewellery, the groom, their attitude everything seems to be wonderful. Lucky girl Sahana.

Shreedevi: Ya Shashi. We are lucky. Hope Alisha also finds someone like Anurag.

Shashikala (Keeps mum for a while and says): A simple guy is enough for us. We have ample wealth.

(And Shashikala diverts everyone towards the sarees)

People enjoy all the ceremonies of the marriage and Alisha observes Sahana's in-laws and compares her would-be in-laws with them.

One day when all the friends had gathered-

Alisha: Hey, Sahana, di's marriage was fantabulous. Enjoyed all the ceremonies.

Sania: Ya, it was just like a celebrity's destination wedding, wow! Loved it.

Alisha: I want my wedding to be super fantastic just like hers.

Maheshwari: Ya -ya, surely it will be as you are the only daughter of Mr. Shailesh Agarwal.

Mohit: Hmmm yeah, rich people have a destination wedding. We poor have a highway wedding. (Everyone laughs.)

Rahul: Okay, you and Sania should get married right here on this highway now.

Mohit: Hey, I was just kidding, man.

Alisha: My wedding will be the most expensive one of the years.

Rahul: Jokes apart. A wedding is not meant to be expensive but rather beautiful.

Alisha: A wedding is a once-in-a-lifetime event, and I want everything to be perfect for mine.

Rahul: A wedding represents the union of two families; it is not simply a business transaction.

Alisha: Hey Rahul, can you also get me the diamond set and lehenga from Sabyasachi?

Rahul: Let us see once the time comes.

Alisha: I understand that you probably won't.

Rahul: Alisha, let's not discuss this right now. Your sister's wedding is over, and we enjoyed it. Why are you comparing your wedding to hers? You are both different.

Alisha: I know I won't be able to receive everything that she got from her in-laws.

Rahul: Alisha, stop behaving like a kid. We are mature individuals. Why are you so inclined towards a lavish life? Can't you see the other way around?

Alisha: Please stop lecturing me.

Alisha leaves the place.

Rahul (to Mohit): Mohit, I don't know if I will ever be able to satisfy her.

Mohit: Take it easy! Let her be alone for a while. She will return to normal.

Rahul: Mohit, you don't know her, man. I have been with her for the past three years, and I understand every bit of her.

Mohit: Rahul, you're overthinking. Just give her some space for a while; she'll be okay.

Rahul: I guess you are right.

Rahul is so madly in love with Alisha that he fulfills all her demands, but she is never satisfied with him. She enjoys being with him but expects a lot of materialistic things. Four years just flew by, and one fine day, it so happens that Rahul takes Alisha for a long drive and stops. He takes her to the garden.

Rahul: Hey Alisha, I want to gift you something very special.

Alisha (Excited): I am curious to see. Show me the gift.

Rahul: Close your eyes.

Rahul confidently puts a gold necklace around her neck and proposes to her, declaring his intention to marry her.

Rahul: Alisha, Will you marry me? I love you.

Alisha gets shocked and suddenly takes the necklace off.

Alisha: Rahul, first, I expected gifts like a diamond locket, a platinum ring, or at least a branded handbag from you. This necklace is gold and has a very traditional design. I can't wear it. I am sorry. And marriage, come on, Rahul. I am only 25 years old. I am not ready to get married. I have ambitions, and I need to fulfil them.

Rahul: I'm sorry. I'll get you the diamond locket next time. We can fulfil our wishes by supporting each other, Alisha.

Alisha: I need some time, Rahul. I don't want my life to be wrapped in the traditions of a typical married Indian woman. I want to enjoy this age as a bachelorette. Please try to understand.

Rahul: I have a job; you have a job what else do you need? My parents are not like typical in-laws. You can do anything that you wish.

Alisha: Please give me 2 to 3 years, and I won't ask you much. Please.........

Rahul: Ok.

And they happily go back.

Rahul goes back home to Jaipur. Rahul's mother talks to him.

Neeta: When are you both planning to marry Rahul? It has been seven years since your relationship began.

Rahul: Mom, she needs some time.

Neeta: But....

Rahul: It's ok. I want to tell you something.

Neeta: Yes, please.

Rahul: I am planning to go to the US.

Neeta: What!!! Are you serious? And why do you have to go to the US?

Rahul: I passed one of the entrance exams at California University but was not planning to go. As Alisha needs 2 to 3 years, I, too, would like to complete my studies.

Neeta: You completed your studies in a prestigious institute in India, and you are in a good position today. You could also do your master's here.

Rahul: I don't want to stay here. I want to go outside for a while.

Neeta: I know Alisha is responsible for all this. She is ruining our life.

Rahul: No, Mom, it is my decision. Please don't blame her.

Neeta (to her husband Karan): Look here, Karan. I sometimes feel this girl is not a good match for him.

Karan: He wants to study abroad. Let him go ahead. It's ok. Don't worry. They can decide their life. It's their right. Leave him. Please don't bring her in between.

Neeta: Ok. But after 2 years you should come back and marry her.

Rahul: Ya, I promise.

Karan: I support your decision, Rahul. It's your life. But please make wise decisions and we are always there for you. Start preparing for your journey. All the best.

Rahul: Thanks, Dad.

Neeta: But don't settle down there.

Rahul: No, Mom, I will be back.

Rahul informs Alisha about his travel.

Rahul: Alisha, I am going to the US for further studies in a month or so.

Alisha (shocked for a moment): But why do you suddenly have to go to the US?

Rahul: I passed the GRE and want to continue my studies. As you said, you still want 2 to 3 years; I would like to pursue higher studies and will come back. Don't worry.

Alisha: But you could have stayed here with me and completed your masters here. Why are you going so far? Leaving me alone here.

Rahul: Alisha, I have been with you for 7+ years and have fulfilled all your desires. I wanted to take you along with me, so I proposed to you. It's ok. We can get married later. But please let me fulfil my desire.

Alisha (little confused): Ok. All the best, but please come soon.

Alisha informs her parents.

Shashikala: Are you mad? You could have gone with him after getting married in a small ceremony.

Alisha: Mom, Marriage is the biggest event in life. Look at Sahana di's marriage. I want to get married just like her.

Shashikala: Marriage is not about how you do it. It's about how you live with your partner and his family.

Alisha: Mom, you also talk like Rahul. Oh my God! I can't take this anymore. I am leaving. Dad, please make her understand.

Shailesh: Everyone should get married. Let her enjoy 2 to 3 years more. How does it matter?

Shashikala: It matters. I felt that Rahul was not happy with her decision. This is why he is immediately flying to the US. This girl annoys him. I don't know about his wealth but he is a good human being. And I don't want her to lose him because of her idiotic and impractical nature.

Shailesh: You are overthinking. He won't leave her. He loves her to the moon and black.

Shashikala: I am not overthinking. I am just thinking but you are not thinking at all. You better think about her.

Shashikala leaves.

And the days pass.

Rahul informs all his friends about his studies. All are sad, especially Mohit.

Mohit: You could have stayed with us, man. I will miss you, friend.

Rahul: I would miss you too.

Maltesh and all his other friends want to arrange a party before he leaves India. All the friends, including Alisha, attend the party. Alisha is a little sad.

Rahul heads to the US and within a short span, Mohit and Sania get engaged as both of their parents are eager to get them married.

Rahul (To Mohit): Congratulations bhai.

Mohit: Thank you. I want you to come over here. Postponing my marriage for you.

Rahul: I'll come and meet you. Don't postpone it.

Mohit: No Rahul. I'll wait for you.

Rahul: Ok. I'll come.

Mohit: How is it between you and Alisha?

Rahul: It is going pretty well.

Mohit: All the best buddy. Do well. See you soon.

After a couple of days

Alisha starts ignoring Rahul's calls and is not available most of the time. Rahul doesn't understand her behaviour and keeps mum for some time. Once Rahul calls her it is a video call. She answers and talks to him for 2 to 5 minutes. Later she becomes uninterested.

Rahul: Hey Alisha. How are you?

Alisha: Hey Rahul, I miss you so much.

Rahul: You seem to be busy nowadays.

Alisha: No Rahul. Just having some work pressure.

Rahul: Ok. Then what's up?

Alisha: Nothing Rahul. I have an important meeting. Can we talk later?

Rahul: Ok dear. Go ahead. We can talk later. Bye, see you.

Alisha: Bye.

She cuts the call.

Alisha (To herself): Finally, I stopped the man.

Shashikala listens to her behind the door.

Shashikala (Knocks on the door): May I come in Alisha?

Alisha: Yes Mom.

Shashikala: Can we talk?

Alisha: Yes, Mom, sure. What do you want to talk about?

Shashikala: You might feel that I am intervening in your personal life. But as a mother, I need to know.

Alisha: Mom, please come to the point.

Shashikala: I see that your relationship with Rahul is taking a different turn. You don't talk to him properly and avoid his calls. What is going on Alisha?

Alisha (hesitating): It is nothing.

Shashikala: Are you serious about this relationship or not?

Alisha: Mom, I just want to enjoy my life before getting married. Rahul is going to be with me anyway, for the rest of my life.

Shashikala: What do you mean? Didn't you enjoy your life? You are 26 years old now. Don't you have any responsibility towards your relationship? Remember one thing, once he starts avoiding you, it won't be easy for you anymore.

Alisha: Mom, take a chill pill. He is only mine. Don't you see how desperate he is to call me? He won't leave me for sure. I have known him for the past 8 years.

Shashikala: Alisha, dear, don't be under the illusion that he doesn't hate you. Remember, he has been tolerating your tantrums for 8 years. You better be careful.

Alisha ignores her and walks away.

Rahul does not understand Alisha's state of mind and continues with his studies.

He does well in his course and makes many friends in the US.

He has some Indian friends in the US. One of his Indian friends asks him about his relationship. Rahul replies, "My relationship is doing well, thank you."

He has a friend named Jessica, who is also Indian. She has always liked Rahul for his attitude and appreciated him.

Once while having a conversation, at the cafe.

Jessica: Hey Rahul, we have been friends for a while now.

Rahul: Yes, I am aware of it.

Jessica: I know many things about you now. Shall I ask you something personal?

Rahul: Yes. You can.

Jessica: I know you have a girlfriend. Are you happy in your relationship?

Rahul: Ya. I am happy. Why this sudden question?

Jessica: No. I just saw you being upset with your girlfriend. So, I thought of asking you this.

Rahul: She is a little cranky but I love her.

Jessica: I can see that. But some people around you also love you.

Rahul: Like?

Jessica: Your friends.

Rahul: Which friends? (Curiously)

Jessica: Can't you see?

Rahul (He looks straight into her eyes): Yes, I can see the one who likes me.

Jessica (Starts looking at the other side): Okay, let us go now. We have had enough talk.

Jessica starts going.

Rahul: Stop Jessi.

Jessica: Now, what?

Rahul: Can't we love each other as friends and remain best friends forever?

Jessica (Starts crying): Yes. Of course.

Rahul: Thank you, my bestie.

Rahul's best friends in the US are Manish, Vipul, and Jessica. Manish also likes Jessica.

Here, Mohit goes to Alisha's home to invite them to his marriage. He invites them. Meanwhile, Alisha gets a call from her friend. Shashikala gets an opportunity to talk to Mohit and asks about Rahul's well-being.

Shashikala: How are you, Mohit? Getting ready for your wedding?

Mohit: Yes Mam. Kind of.

Shashikala: Invited all your friends? How about Rahul?

Mohit: He is the reason I postponed my wedding for 6 months.

Shashikala: I understand. You both have been together since school days, right? Your bonding is strong.

Mohit: Yes. He is my friend, partner in crime, etc.

Shashikala: Can I ask you something? If you don't mind?

Mohit: Yes mam. Of course.

Shashikala: Is Rahul happy with Alisha? I don't know what's going on between them. I see that she has been avoiding his calls, and I'm worried about it. You are his best friend. He might have shared something. I don't want Rahul to leave her, as she is a little cranky.

Mohit: No worries mam. I will talk to Rahul and get back to you. But he hasn't shared any such thing with me.

Shashikala: This is not the right time to bother you but………

Mohit: It's fine mam. I'll take your leave. Do attend the wedding and shower your blessings on us.

Shashikala: Yes sure. All the best dear Mohit.

And Mohit leaves.

Mohit speaks to Rahul and invites him. Also invites his parents separately.

Rahul travels to India to attend his best friend Mohit's wedding. Five days before the wedding, Rahul and his parents go to Mohit's place. Alisha arrives with her mother. Shashikala waves to him and asks Alisha to speak to him.

Alisha: Hi, Rahul. Nice to see you after a year. How are you, sweetheart? I missed you so much.

Rahul: Hey Alisha, you always seem to be busy dear.

Alisha: You know how it is in the companies; I need to handle pressure.

Rahul: Ya, I understand. It's fine. Let us go on a date. It's been a very long time.

Alisha: Ya sure.

Mohit is carefully observing these two.

Mohit: I'll be back in a moment.

Sania: Ok. Where are you going?

Mohit: I am marrying to be with you only. I just want to talk to Rahul.

Sania: Don't disturb them. Let them spend some quality time.

Mohit: Oh really!

Sania: What has happened to you?

Mohit: I'll tell you later.

Mohit goes and talks to Rahul and Alisha.

Mohit: Hey love birds.

Rahul: Go and sit with your bird.

Mohit: Oye. I want to spend some time with my school buddy. I will disturb you both for a very short period. Alisha, please don't mind.

Alisha: You always do. I won't let you be peaceful on your first night.

Mohit: Oye, Alisha, don't do that. I will take revenge on you.

Alisha: I'll see to it.

Meanwhile, Vinay arrives and waves to Alisha.

Vinay: Hey Alisha.

Alisha (Excited): Hi Vinay.

Alisha to Rahul and Mohit: I'll catch you guys in a moment, please.

Mohit doesn't like it.

Rahul: Why are you so furious?

Mohit: Leave it. Just tell me one thing. Has Alisha been avoiding your calls lately? Is everything okay between you?

Rahul: Ya, she had been a little occupied recently. Who told you?

Mohit: Shashi mam told me. She was worried about your relationship and I think Alisha was not responding to her properly.

Rahul: Oh, that's okay. I don't think there is any problem. Maybe she was busy with some important work or projects.

Mohit: I hope so.

Rahul: Who is that guy?

Mohit: Vinay, her colleague.

Rahul: Ok. But why did you look at them furiously?

Mohit: She is getting close to him nowadays.

Rahul: That's fine. I, too, have girls as my friends in the US.

Mohit: Rahul, I don't want to intervene in your personal life. I know how much you love her, but nowadays, she is not as into you, as you are.

Rahul: I don't think so.

Mohit: I just want the best for you.

Rahul: Thank you.

All the friends enjoy the marriage ceremonies, such as dance and mehendi, and after five days, Mohit and Sania get married.

Rahul spends a few weeks at his hometown and one day asks Alisha for a date.

Rahul: Shall we go on a dinner date?

Alisha: Ya. I am waiting for it.

Rahul takes Alisha on a dinner date before leaving for the US.

Rahul: What do you think about marriage?

Alisha: I said to you earlier that I need a bit more time.

Rahul: I did not specify anything. But anyway, I shall wait for you.

Alisha: I know that.

Suddenly Rahul gets Jessica's call.

Jessica: Hey, I have something to tell you. I hope I am not disturbing you.

Rahul: You are so excited just let me know.

Jessica: I am in a relationship. Guess who?

Rahul: Manish?

Jessica: How did you guess man?

Rahul: I guessed the way he looked at you all the time.

Jessica: He proposed to me. But your guess was so apt.

Rahul: It was a guess. I hope you got the man of your life.

Jessica: I had a love failure.

Rahul: With whom?

Jessica: With you.

Rahul: Are you still sticking to the same thing?

Jessica: No buddy. I moved on. Otherwise, how could I accept his proposal?

Rahul: I am happy for you Jessi.

Jessica: Can I tell you something?

Rahul: Ya. Go on.

Jessica: I am happy that I got you in the form of a bestie and I love you, buddy.

Rahul: Love you, bestie.

Alisha: Girlfriend in the US?

Rahul: Ya. As if you don't have any male friends. Who is Vinay? I can also be possessive.

Alisha: He is my colleague.

Rahul: She is Jessica. She used to like me, but I rejected her proposal. Now, she is committed to Manish.

Alisha: I see that in the US relationships are common.

Rahul: They are common in India too. But one should have trust. Don't you trust me?

Alisha: I trust you. Just a casual question.

Rahul: I can see everything in your eyes. I have no relationships in the US. I am committed to you.

Alisha: I know you.

Rahul drops her to the house, and before leaving, Shashikala calls him inside.

Shashikala: It's your turn to get married now.

Rahul: Yes Aunty, the very next year. If Alisha agrees.

Shashikala: Both of you are committed. You can get married anytime, and now you can get married and take her to the US.

Rahul: I have waited for so long. One more year doesn't make much difference to me.

Alisha: Mom, I want a lavish wedding. I can't just get married in a small ceremony. After all, I am the only daughter of the Aggarwals.

Shailesh: Why not? She is my only daughter.

Rahul takes a leave and heads back to the US.

He meets all his US friends, including Manish, Vipul, and Jessica. He congratulates Jessica and Manish on their new relationship and they end up having a party.

He shows the wedding pictures of Mohit along with his family and Alisha.

Jessica: Alisha is beautiful.

Rahul: Thank you, bestie.

Manish: When are you going to introduce her to us?

Rahul: Very soon.

After 1 year.

Rahul heads back to India. His family is happy. Alisha is out of India on a trip to Europe with her friends. He takes up a job in India. There a team of interns who join under Rahul. Vidya, Varun, Meera, Nidhi, and Siddarth.

There are these two senior guys, Danesh and Raj, who constantly flirt with girls. Vidya is working under Danesh, who constantly stares at her. He

doesn't teach her any work but asks her favours instead.

Vidya: Sir, I have been working on this project for a month now. I need your approval for the presentation that I made.

Danesh: We will see it. I need to talk to you personally tonight. Meet me at the Malabar Café.

Vidya: Sir, can we talk here?

Danesh: If you want the approval do as I say.

Vidya: I'll think about it.

Vidya leaves and the other interns and Rahul watch them. While having lunch Rahul calls all the interns and asks Vidya about her problem. Vidya tells him everything that happened. The other girl, Nidhi, also complains the same thing about Raj. Before they talk further, Danesh and Raj arrive. They immediately stop the conversation and change the topic.

A week passes, and the company arranges a trip. All the interns and employees get ready for it. The trip is to understand the IT companies in Bangalore. They collaborated with some companies in Bangalore. There is a conference and a party was arranged.

All the interns go on the trip and are excited. Rahul, along with the other employees, are happy to arrange the trip. Danesh and Raj are excited to flirt with the girls. They arrange a bus and start the trip with different games like Antakshari. Danesh and Raj are trying to be very nice to the girls. Rahul is taking

care of the conference and the trip administration. They reach Bangalore. The next day a conference is arranged where the industry experts would address the topic "How to address the real challenges of an employee in an IT Company." The next day in the conference

Industry Expert Devang Malhotra, along with Mahesh Shinde, Neelam Jaiswal, and Varun Mehta, addresses the conference.

Devang Malhotra (Loudly): Hi Techies,

Audience (Chorus): Hello Sir,

Devang Malhotra: I Welcome you all to the conference on- How to address the real challenges of an employee in an IT Company.

Now, I would like to know from the employees: What kind of IT challenges do you face? Is anybody facing any such challenge?

Raghu raises his hand.

Raghu: Sir, my name is Raghu. I have been working on a project for the last three years, and the resources allocated are way too little compared to what we require. We are facing challenges with completing the project in the stipulated period, as I and the other guy are responsible for the whole project. The whole project is dependent on us now. How do we deal with these kinds of challenges?

Devang Malhotra: Hi, Raghu. It is a wonderful question. According to this problem, you are facing challenges regarding Resource management. How many years of work experience do you have?

Raghu: Around 6 years sir.

Devang Malhotra: Okay. You people mainly deal with software implementation and support projects. Sometimes, they are infra-related. Are there any other challenges?

Rahul: Sir, I am Rahul. How to deal with the knowledge management problem?

Devang Malhotra: This is one of the major problems that we deal with while working on the project. Most of the time, this is not considered a major problem, but it should not be ignored. Employees should put their knowledge into the project to make it successful.

Our resource allocation should go hand in hand with the knowledge the employee has because it is teamwork. Now, the issue that both of you brought forward indicates management problems, which will be dealt with by Ms. Neelam after the break.

Coming to the core IT problems

I will deal with the server and error-handling challenges in the afternoon today. In the evening, Ms. Neelam will take over the Resource Management and Knowledge Management challenges. Is that OK, guys?

Audience: Yes sir.

Devang Malhotra: Okay. Now, have a lunch break. I'll catch up with you guys after one hour.

All the people leave for the lunch.

During lunchtime, Danesh and Raj are constantly staring at the interns.

Danesh: These intern girls are too cute.

Raj: Yes, I am bored of seeing our office girls. At least for a few days, we can witness something fresh.

Danesh: Look at Vidya, she is so very cute.

Raj: Hey, she is working under you. Did something happen between you?

Danesh: No. She is stubborn. I tried a lot. But…

Raj: It's fine. Keep trying man.

Rahul, with his colleagues and the interns, have lunch.

After the break, the main conference starts with Devang Malhotra.

Devang Malhotra: Welcome, guys. I hope you had a good lunch today. I know it is a bit tiring, but I promise to make it a joyful session for you all. Let us not make this a monotonous presentation. I want good interaction with you. Shall we begin?

Audience: Yes sir.

Devang Malhotra: I am Devang Malhotra. I have 20 years of experience in IT. I served as a techie for 15 years and was in engineering management for 5 years. I have encountered many challenges over time. I am happy to give you input and answer as many questions as possible.

Let us begin the session now.

I work with error handling and server problems in the IT industry. Let's first understand the types of errors we get.

Hardware, Communication, Runtime, Functional, Syntax, Server, and many more types of errors that we come across.

He continued the session for about two and a half hours and then handed it over to Manish Shinde, Neelam Jaiswal, and Varun Mehta.

After the tea break, they start the evening session.

Ms Neelam Jaiswal takes over.

Neelam: Hello, my dears. How are you? I hope you all are doing well. My name is Neelam Jaiswal, and I am the resource person for management issues in the IT sector. I am a postgraduate in management science and have 15 years of experience in IT. For the past 7 years, I have been serving as a manager in the service sector.

Now, let us understand the managerial issues raised by you people during the orientation session.

Resource allocation and knowledge management play vital roles for managers. We are going to discuss accurate planning, including employees in varied tasks, motivating the right employees, and placing them on the right projects.

Neelam assigns one task to Danesh and Vidya as she is working under Danesh along with some other interns and managers.

She continues the session for 2 and a half hours and wishes them the best for their future.

Danesh: Hey Vidya, the assigned project should be submitted in 15 days. Come on, let's go and discuss it.

Vidya (Hesitant): Sir we can discuss it later.

Manoj Shinde comes and asks all the interns to go with their managers for the project as they have all the resources available.

All the interns go with their respective managers to discuss the project assigned to them along with Nidhi and Raj, Vidya, and Danesh.

Everyone starts working in different locations. Some sit in the conference room, and some walk around. Danesh takes Vidya to one of the small conference rooms.

Danesh: Hey, Vidya, you look hot today.

Vidya (Anxious): Sir, let's discuss the project. We have many videos, PowerPoints, and books available.

She goes near the table to search the books suitable for the project. Danesh slowly walks, immediately locks the door, and grabs her from the back. She tries to push him and pushes him with force. Furious Danesh again grabs and sexually assaults her.

She cries in deep, and Danesh warns her not to talk about this incident with anyone; otherwise, he would blacklist her. She immediately leaves the conference room. While leaving the room, Rahul watches her

and suspects something. But Vidya pretends to be normal and goes.

The next day they are supposed to return to Mumbai. After returning to Mumbai, Vidya cannot focus on her work and Rahul constantly observes her. One fine day, Rahul takes her to the café and asks her.

Rahul: Vidya, what is wrong with you? I can see some abnormal changes in your behavior. You can share it with me.

Vidya (Hesitant): Sir, there is nothing wrong with me.

After asking her repeatedly she finally cries.

Rahul: Did Danesh do something?

Vidya: He spoiled my life. I don't want to live. I can't face my parents. I can't face myself. I broke up with my fiancée who was my long-term boyfriend. I have nothing to live for.

Vidya leaves the café.

Rahul immediately goes to the office to meet Danesh.

Rahul: What happened between you and Vidya in the Bangalore conference hall?

Danesh: Nothing buddy! Did she tell you something?

Rahul: It doesn't matter what she says. I could see her coming out of the conference hall and her physical and mental state wasn't normal.

Danesh: See Rahul, I don't want to drag the things. Everything is normal between us. I know that she is trying to create a fuss.

Rahul: Is that so?

Danesh: Chill buddy! You know it happens between two people. It happened between us. It happened with her consent.

Rahul: Why are you being so casual? I know how you are. She cannot give you the consent to touch her.

Danesh: Hey Rahul, you just stay out of it man. She is a bloody slut... (Rahul slaps him and goes.)

Rahul goes to Vidya's house.

The scenario is horrible. Vidya's parents are petrified as she breaks her engagement with her long-term boyfriend. Vidya's father (Jainesh) opens the door for Rahul.

Rahul: Hello! Uncle.

Jainesh: Who are you now? What do you want from us?

Rahul: I am Vidya's senior.

Jainesh: What do you want? What else has happened with her?

Rahul: Sir, I am very well aware of the incident. Can I meet her?

Jainesh: We are getting her married. We have decided to get her married.

Rahul: Sir, once let me talk to her, please.

Jainesh: Mr. Rahul. I don't want any further consequences in her life. Please don't try to meet her. She has already spoiled her life by working in your IT company. She broke up with her fiancée. She chose him. We agreed. But now, I don't want anyone to even talk to her. I humbly request you to go away from here now.

Rahul: Ok.

Rahul leaves the house.

At night, Rahul calls Vidya.

Vidya: Hello sir.

Rahul: How are you?

Vidya(crying): Not good.

Rahul: I understand, and I am aware of what happened. I'm sorry for the breakup. I don't know how to help you.

Vidya: You don't have to help. My parents have already decided to get me married. They have found the solution.

Rahul: Who is the guy? Do you know him?

Vidya: He is a 50-year-old guy. He is a businessman. He needs a wife.

Rahul: But how can you agree to this? This is not fair to you.

Vidya: It's my fate. I can't change this.

Rahul: No. Please listen to me. Can I talk to your fiancée? Maybe I could explain him.

Vidya: No Sir. I tried a lot but he thinks I am not suitable for him any longer .

Rahul: Don't worry. I will see, if I can do something for you.

Vidya: I don't think anybody can help me. My parents are shattered. I don't want to hurt them anymore. I am accepting the things now.

Rahul: Ok. Now you get relaxed. We will see tomorrow. Bye, take good care.

Vidya's engagement is fixed with an old guy. After two days, Vidya gets engaged in a small ceremony. Her fiancée tries to be close to her, but she gets uncomfortable. She calls Rahul.

Vidya: Hello Sir, I am devastated. I don't understand why things are going this way.

Rahul: What happened Vidya?

Vidya: I am engaged to Mr. Raval. I am not comfortable with him and don't know how I will accept him.

Rahul: Tell your parents that you can't accept him

Vidya: I don't have a choice. I should listen to them.

Rahul: Let me come and talk to them.

Vidya: No, sir, it's not required. I just wanted to share with someone, and as you are aware of my situation, I told you. Thank you for listening to me.

Soon Jainesh arrives and snatches the phone from her.

Jainesh: Listen to me, Vidya. You have done enough and I cannot tolerate this now. Somebody is giving you the life despite knowing the situation and you don't even want to talk to him. I asked apology from him on your behalf. Now, no more tantrums.

You are so fortunate to marry him and he has forgiven you this time. Talk to him and cooperate with us.

Are you again talking to the same guy Rahul?

Vidya: No, I stopped talking to everyone. I'll listen to you from now on.

Jainesh: That's better.

Vidya's mother, Ujwala, tries to console her and asks Jainesh if Vidya can buy more time for the marriage. But Jainesh refuses and asks Ujwala to prepare her daughter for the marriage.

A week goes by and Rahul tries to contact Vidya. But her phone is switched off.

On the marriage day, Vidya faints during the rituals. She is taken to the hospital and the doctor says that she swallowed the sleeping pills.

Now, Jainesh and Ujwala are shocked. Ujwala suggests Jainesh to call Rahul.

Jainesh finds Rahul's number and calls him. He informs him about the situation and asks him to visit her.

Rahul arrives at the hospital with 2 of his friends. The doctor says that she is doing better now. One of the family members can meet her and Rahul goes inside.

Rahul: How are you?

Vidya: I don't know.

Rahul (Calls his friends from outside and her parents): Vidya, I need your signatures on this paper.

Vidya: What is this?

Rahul: I'll tell you later.

Vidya: But……

Rahul: Just sign I say. Don't ask me anything now.

She signs.

Rahul signs on the same paper and says…

Vidya, you are legally my wife.

I'll get your discharge papers and you will move with me.

She is dumbstruck and gets discharged, and Rahul takes her to her house with her parents. She packs her bag. Meanwhile…

Jainesh (With tears in his eyes joining his hands): I don't know what to say, Mr. Rahul. But thank you from the bottom of my heart.

Rahul: You don't have to thank me, sir. I did what I felt right at that moment.

Ujwala: You are a great human being. God bless you son.

Rahul takes Vidya along with him to his rented apartment.

For quite a while, they don't talk to each other. Vidya sits and looks outside the window. After some time, Rahul goes inside the room and starts talking to her.

Rahul: I should have spoken to you about my decision. I am sorry that this sudden decision has left you shocked.

Vidya: You don't need to be sorry. Whatever you did was for me and my life. But you are committed. Now, what is your next plan?

Rahul: I still love Alisha. I'll try to convince her and ask her sometime. I need to get you settled first.

Vidya: I do understand. Thank you. I have the highest respect for you.

Rahul is baffled by life situations. He calls Mohit.

Rahul: Hi Mohit, how are you, buddy?

Mohit: I am fine. How are you?

Rahul: I am good. Can you come over here?

Mohit: Any emergency?

Rahul: Kind of.

Mohit: Ok. I'll be there in half an hour.

Mohit informs Sania about the emergency and meets Rahul.

Mohit at Rahul's apartment.

Mohit: But what about Alisha? Did you think of her? How would you sustain her?

Rahul: She might return from Europe anytime this week. Shashi mam informed me.

Mohit: Ok. Just take care of Vidya. She has been through a lot. I'll think of something. You don't take stress.

Rahul: Ok.

The very next week, Alisha returns from Europe. She instantly learns that Rahul is married to Vidya, and she goes to his apartment.

Alisha (very furious): Hey Rahul, are you cheating on me? What is all this nonsense? I was just hanging out with my friends, and meanwhile, you started dating the other girl and got married!

Rahul: Calm down. Let me explain….

Alisha: No. I need an answer.

Rahul explains the situation in which he got married.

Alisha: You mean to say that if any random girl is a rape victim, you are going to marry her. Right. She is not the only girl, there are many others. The victims of domestic violence, and acid attack victims, go and get married to everyone. Just go.

Rahul: You have lost your mind. Go home. I'll talk to you again.

Alisha: Let me at least see the girl. I'll screw her life. Where is that bloody girl?

Rahul: Look! She has gone through a lot, don't create a scene here.

Alisha is so furious that she bangs the table and starts beating Rahul. Rahul calls Shashikala and asks her to take Alisha home. Shashikala apologizes and takes her back home.

Vidya realizes that she created a big mess in Rahul's life and starts crying. But Rahul consoles her.

While going back home, Alisha asks her mother.

Alisha: Mom, why didn't you tell me this earlier?

Shashikala: What do you expect me to say? I asked you to contact him after going to Europe. You are so busy in your world that you don't even understand how the other person feels. You are in a relationship, and you don't even know how sensitive it is. Everything is taken for granted by you. Don't ask me such questions. Better try to improve yourself.

Alisha: So now, you mean to say that I made the greatest mistake of my life, and I am going to lose him? What did I do? Is enjoyment with friends a crime? Is being myself a crime? Asking for some time to get married is a crime?

Shashikala: No, you can enjoy with your friends, ask for time. But you did not value the person or the relationship. You ignored his calls. You did not give him time. Roaming with your colleague Vinay. Don't you think it's wrong? You are grown up now. Try to analyze yourself.

After going home,

Alisha goes to her father and cries.

Shailesh: I am going to screw his life now. What does he think of himself?

Shashikala: You both are proud of your power and money. You didn't teach your daughter the relationship values. She is a rich, spoiled kid. Remember Alisha, I told you that once he starts avoiding you, you won't be able to tolerate it.

Shashikala leaves.

Here, Rahul has to go to his hometown. He doesn't understand how to deal with his parents, but he takes Vidya along with him anyway.

At his residence, his parents are shocked to know.

Neeta: Have you gone mad Rahul? I wasn't interested in Alisha, but we agreed on your happiness. Now, Vidya. I don't understand you. You are spoiling our lives. Do you understand the impact of this on Disha's life? You don't understand.

Karan: This time, I stand beside your mother. You could have informed us. After all, we are your parents. I support all your decisions. But now don't expect me to do that.

Vidya is chatting with his sister outside.

At night, Neeta doesn't like Vidya. But serves the food to everyone. Karan doesn't react.

After the dinner,

Rahul is standing in his balcony.

Disha: Hey brother.

Rahul: Hey Dish.

Disha: I support your decision for Vidya. I stand beside you. Don't worry about me.

Rahul: Thank you so much.

In the next two days, Rahul leaves his hometown and heads back to Mumbai.

He meets Alisha in a restaurant.

Rahul: Alisha, I am sorry for whatever happened.

Alisha: When are you going to marry me?

Rahul: Remember, When I asked you this question, you borrowed 2 years or even more. Now I want the same thing from you. I'll get her settled and will marry you.

Alisha: Ok. I trust you.

They go to their respective homes.

Rahul starts working and starts his regular life.

The scars of the past incidents prevent Vidya from going ahead in life.

She often sits and watches outside the window. Rahul understands that she needs some change.

He decides to take her to the US for a while, so that her mind settles and she becomes stable. They apply for her visa. He applies for a job, and he already has a student Visa. The company sponsors his visa, and she somehow gets the dependent visa. They fly to the US in six months. He informs his parents, Mohit, Alisha, and Vidya's parents, that he will return from the US after a while.

After reaching the US, they have an apartment.

Rahul: Vidya, feel yourself comfortable here. I have some known friends here .

Vidya: Ok. You left India because of me. You wanted to stay there, marry Alisha, and settle yourself there. I created a lot of havoc in your life.

Rahul: I decided to marry you. Settle your life. It is solely my responsibility. You don't have to feel guilty. Chill!!

Ok. I called some of my friends here. They will be your friends, too, and they will be here soon. Get ready.

Vidya and Rahul get ready and his friends Manish, Jessica, and Vipul arrive.

Rahul: Hey buddies, missed you a lot in India.

Manish: We missed you too.

Jessica (comforts Vidya): Vidya, you are beautiful. By the way, I am Jessica. Rahul's bestie.

Manish: I am Manish.

Vipul: I am Vipul.

Vipul: Hey Vidya, if you need anything we are just one call away from you.

Manish: Yes, and Rahul believe me, Vidya will soon get adjusted to the US.

Vidya smiles comfortably for the first time in a long while. Seeing her smile, Rahul feels that his decision was the right one.

Rahul: Sorry guys, I couldn't prepare anything for you. I'll bring some snacks.

Jessica: You people have just arrived, and we must help you with the drinks and snacks. I couldn't prepare anything this time, but let's go to an Italian restaurant. Vidya, do you like it? Or do you have any other preferences?

Vidya: I am ok with anything.

Jessica: Rahul, I won't ask your preferences, you know that.

Rahul: I know that, Jessi. Whatever you prefer.

They go to an Italian restaurant. They have lunch together and chit-chat.

After the lunch, Jessica and Rahul go and get some drinks.

Jessica: I can imagine that things have been challenging for you, Rahul, and I want you to know that I appreciate you for handling it all. I'm curious about your relationship with Alisha—how are things going between you two?

Rahul: I managed to convince her to settle Vidya, and then marry her. I requested some time.

Jessica: That's good. I hope everything will happen as expected.

Rahul: Ya, I do hope.

Vipul: Did you guys order some drinks

Rahul: Yes, one beer and two whiskies.

Vipul: Come on let's go and wait there.

Rahul: Ok. Let us go.

After lunch, everyone leaves and returns to their respective homes.

Rahul and Vidya take a short break. Rahul then goes to buy some groceries.

Rahul: I got the required groceries.

Vidya: Ok, sir.

Rahul (Makes a weird face): Look I am your husband.

Vidya looked on with a confused expression.

Rahul: Okay, friends? Let's be friends from today onwards.

Vidya: Ok. Sir.

Rahul: No more, sir. Am I your boss? Is this a company where you work? Just call me Rahul.

Vidya: Ok. Rahul.

They shake hands.

Rahul: Do you know cooking?

Vidya: I have some knowledge about it, but I will do my best to learn more.

Rahul: We both will cook something today for dinner.

They sit for a while and talk to each other.

Rahul: What do you want to do in the US? Do you want to study something or would you like to work?

Vidya: I don't know.

Rahul: Sometime back in India, you said you wanted to get certified in Animation. Do you still want to pursue that ?

Vidya: I don't want to impose on you. I'll find a job.

Rahul: There's no need to worry about financing. Many options are available. You can work and learn, or I can assist you. It's not difficult.

Vidya: Ok.

Rahul opens the website on his laptop to know the universities offering the Animation programs.

Rahul: Various certifications and master's degrees are available. Take a look and decide which university you would like to attend. We can then check the requirements and other details.

Vidya: I believe California University offers a Master's program in Design and Animation, and I am interested.

Rahul: Let's apply and review the requirements. I believe there is an entrance exam and the GRE. Begin your preparations for it.

Vidya: Are you certain about this? Is it possible for me to proceed?

Rahul: Absolutely certain.

At night-

Rahul: I'll cook something for us. You just relax today.

Vidya: No, I'll take care of that.

Rahul: Okay, we both can prepare something together.

Both Rahul and Vidya prepare dinner and get along well with each other. Vidya starts studying for the entrance examination, and after putting in a lot of hard work, she successfully clears it. As a result, she gains admission to California University for a Master's program in Designing and Animation. During this time, her bond with her friends grows stronger. She travels to the university and focuses on her studies.

One fine day, Vidya tells Rahul- I want to visit different places in the U.S. Shall we plan a trip this time? It's my vacation.

Rahul replies, Yeah, sure! Where do you want to go?

Vidya responds, Los Angeles.

Rahul exclaims, "That's a great choice! The city is always vibrant. Let's plan it for this weekend."

Vidya expressed, I hope I'm not causing you any inconvenience. Rahul encouraged her, saying, Get ready for the trip; I'm really glad to see you moving forward in life.

Together with Jessica, Manish, and Vipul, Vidya and Rahul looked forward to an exciting adventure. In Los Angeles, they embraced the vibrant atmosphere, dancing and celebrating. Rahul and Vidya particularly enjoyed their time dancing together, creating memorable moments. However, amidst the fun, Rahul remembered his commitment to Alisha.

Upon their return, Alisha called Rahul. While their conversation was brief, it reflected her feelings. Alisha soon found herself reflecting on her mother's words: "Once he starts avoiding you, it will be hard to bear." That thought sparked something within her, and although she sensed Rahul's growing distance, she focused on self-soothing.

At the same time, Mohit found an exciting opportunity to travel to the US for a project, presenting a chance for personal and professional growth.

Mohit calls Rahul.

Mohit: Hey Rahul, how have you been?

Rahul: I've been doing well, thanks! How about you?

Mohit: I'm doing well too. How is Vidya?

Rahul: With God's grace, she's doing great.

Mohit: I have some exciting news to share!

Rahul: Oh really? I'm curious!

Mohit: Yes! I'm coming to the US for a project in the middle of August.

Rahul: That's fantastic! You should stay with us.

Mohit: I'd love to! Thank you for the invitation. Would that work for you?

Rahul: Absolutely, it would be wonderful to have you over!

Mohit: I mean to say if you are occupied with your work. I don't want to disturb you.

Rahul: Oye! You just come here. Don't think otherwise.

Mohit: Ok.

In just a few days, Mohit is set to embark on his journey to the US, an opportunity that promises exciting experiences and new horizons

Mohit arrives in the US, where Rahul warmly welcomes him and takes him to his apartment. To make his arrival even more special, Vidya prepares a delicious breakfast for him.

Mohit: Hi Rahul, I hope you're doing well! How is your work progressing? I'd love to hear about any new projects or challenges you're facing.

Rahul: Everything is going well. Some projects are a bit challenging but manageable. Which project are you currently working on?

Mohit: I am currently working on the mechanical design project. It is interesting but stressful.

Rahul: Get relaxed and freshen up. Vidya has prepared breakfast for you.

Mohit: Ok.

Mohit takes a bath and enjoys breakfast.

Mohit: Vidya, the breakfast is delicious. You cook well.

Vidya: Thank you.

Mohit: By the way how are your studies? Is it interesting?

Vidya: I need to put in some effort but yes, it is interesting.

Mohit: She looks happy. You are taking good care of her Rahul.

Rahul: She is slowly getting acquainted with the US. Eventually, everything is falling into place.

Mohit: That's great to hear.

Rahul: How is Sania? I haven't spoken to her for a long while.

Mohit: She is doing great. We will talk to her in the evening.

Rahul: Would you like to go for a short walk, Mohit?

Mohit: Ya I would love to.

Rahul and Mohit go for a short walk

Mohit: You are taking good care of her.

Rahul: She is strong enough.

Mohit: It wasn't possible without you.

Rahul smiles and after a short walk, they go back home.

Rahul: What would you like to have for lunch?

Mohit: Nothing specific. You know me.

Rahul: Shall we make Aloo sabji and paratha?

Mohit: That is my favorite.

Rahul: Ok. Done.

Vidya studies and helps a bit to Rahul. Mohit and Rahul prepare lunch.

In the evening, they give a video call to Sania

Mohit: Hey Sania, look who is here.

Sania: It must be Rahul.

They engage in casual conversation, and Vidya joins in as well. They enjoy their day together.

Mohit enjoys a great time with Rahul and Vidya.

Meanwhile, Mohit realizes that Rahul is happier than ever. He feels the contentment radiating from him.

Mohit spends two weeks with them, creating lasting memories before he heads back to India.

Vidya is dedicated to her studies and making great progress, while Rahul is engaged in his work and gaining valuable experience.

On the other side, Rahul and Alisha are engaged in a long-distance relationship. While Rahul dedicates sufficient time to Alisha, she nonetheless perceives notable changes in his behavior.

Alisha decisively approaches Vinay and begins to spend more time with him, all while confidently maintaining her relationship with Rahul.

Mohit discovers that Alisha is seeing both Vinay and Rahul at the same time.

Mohit tries to inform Rahul about Alisha. But Rahul believes her blindly.

One day on the call.

Mohit: Hey Rahul.

Rahul: Hi Mohit. Wats up?

Mohit: There is nothing special to say. You speak.

Rahul: Vidya is completely all right and I need to find a suitable partner for her. My responsibility will be over.

Mohit: Who do you think suits her?

Rahul: I should see.

Mohit: The one who understands and stands beside her and knows her situation. I hope you understand.

Rahul (Thinks for a while) Ya I do.

Rahul once asked if he could drop Vidya off at the university. She agrees.

He develops some connection with her.

He again goes to the university to pick her home.

Vidya: I was coming home. It wasn't required for you to come over.

Rahul: I thought we could have some coffee and snacks together.

Vidya: That would be great.

Rahul and Vidya spend some time in a nearby café.

Rahul: I don't know much about your hobbies. What do you like to do in your free time?

Vidya: If this is your question, then I would say it's not a hobby but my life.

Rahul: What is it?

Vidya: It is dance and I love it.

Rahul (Astonished): Is it? I, too, love dancing. I spent a lot of time on it, but after getting into IIT, I stopped.

There is an event going on in the café, and there is a dance floor. One guy comes and forcibly takes all the couples to dance on the floor. He also takes Rahul and Vidya to the dance floor. Vidya initially hesitates, but Rahul told her that If she finds life in dancing, just do it.

Vidya gets motivated by his words and dances with him. They enjoy dancing together.

Later they go back home.

Rahul: If it were your life, I would not have seen you perform during your internship in the company, nor would you have mentioned it to me.

Vidya: My father did not like it from the very beginning. So, I quit.

Rahul: You should resume it. Your dancing skills are good.

Vidya: I'll think about it.

Rahul: We get one life. Do whatever your heart desires.

Vidya: Thank you for motivating me.

Rahul: What shall we cook for lunch today?

Vidya: I shall prepare something.

Rahul: I know that you are still learning to cook. I shall help you.

Vidya: You know me.

Rahul: Obviously.

Once when in the middle of the call with Alisha, Rahul's friendly nature toward Vidya frustrates Alisha.

Alisha: Why are you being so friendly to her?

Rahul: We are friends.

Alisha: There is no need to be friends with her. Send her to a hostel near the university. As you said in our last conversation, she is completely alright.

Rahul: What is the need for a hostel?

Alisha: As you said, before going to the US, your marriage is just a contract to settle her.

Rahul: Yes, I did.

Alisha: I don't want to see her with you in your apartment.

Rahul: Why are you insisting on this? Don't you trust me?

Alisha: Don't ask me anything now. I want her out of the apartment in my next call.

If you need to support her, she doesn't have to stay with you. You can do this by placing her in a hostel.

Rahul: Alright. There's no need to be upset. I'll take some time to consider it.

Alisha: You should do it as soon as possible.

Rahul expresses his concerns during a phone call with Mohit, where he shares details about his conversation with Alisha.

Mohit reaches out to Alisha for an important in-person discussion.

Mohit: Hi Alisha, how have you been?

Alisha: Hi Mohit, I have been good. What about you?

Mohit: I have been good so far.

Alisha: You mentioned there is something important to discuss.

Mohit: Yes.

Alisha: Please let me know.

Mohit: I'll get straight to the point. I would like to discuss Vidya's staying with Rahul.

Alisha: I'll also get straight to the point. Who are you to discuss this?

It is a personal matter between me and Rahul.

Mohit: I understand that Vidya is recovering and it's not a good time to place her in the hostel.

Alisha: Stay out of this, Mohit. Have I ever intervened in your life or Sania's?

Mohit: No.

Alisha: Then leave us.

Alisha leaves the restaurant in a huff. She realizes that there is something more than friendship between Rahul and Vidya, and she needs to put an end to it.

Alisha at her residence.

Alisha: Dad, I would like to visit the US.

Shailesh: Why the sudden shift? What's up with that?

Alisha: Dad, I want to meet Rahul.

Shailesh: Ok. I'll get your tourist visa done. When are you planning the visit?

Alisha: As soon as possible.

Shailesh has many contacts, and within two weeks, she obtains a tourist visa to the U.S.

She surprises Rahul by calling him directly and asking him to pick her up.

Rahul is feeling both happy and anxious. He picks her up from the airport.

Vidya is at the university. Rahul asks her to come on her own, and after some time, Vidya arrives.

Alisha introduces herself.

Alisha: Hi, this is Alisha. Rahul's would-be wife. You are aware of this, right?

Vidya: Yes, I am well aware.

Alisha: How have you been progressing with your studies lately?

Vidya: Yes, I am enjoying it. I am doing well.

Alisha: You must have made a lot of friends at the university.

Vidya: Yes, ample of them.

Alisha: Why do you have to stay here with him? You can go to a nearby hostel with your friends. If you need any financial help, I'll take care of it.

Rahul: We will think about it. What would you like to have?

Vidya: Yes Alisha. I will prepare for you.

Alisha: Alisha!!!!! Really?

Vidya: Did I commit any mistake?

Alisha: What is your age?

Vidya: 25

Alisha: I am 28. Don't you respect the ones older than you?

Vidya: Sorry.

Alisha: Call me Alisha di from today.

Vidya: Ok Alisha di.

Alisha: By this relationship, Rahul becomes your Jiju understood.

Vidya (Nervous): Ok. Alisha di. What would you like to have?

Alisha: This house belongs to me. I'll prepare something for everyone.

Vidya: I'll show you everything.

Alisha: Ok.

Vidya calls Rahul jijaji in front of Alisha, and Rahul goes out for a while and calls Mohit.

Rahul informs Mohit about his situation.

Mohit spoke with his manager about the possibility of being assigned to an onsite project in the United States. He expressed his eagerness for the opportunity, highlighting how it would enhance his skills and benefit the team.

His manager approves.

Mohit (to Sania): I am going to the US.

Sania: You have been there recently.

Mohit: However, this is now for a different purpose.

Sania: For Rahul, is it?

Mohit: Alisha is in the US.

Sania: What!! When did she go there?

Mohit: Last week. She is trying to evacuate Vidya from the apartment. I had never seen him happy so far. Rahul is alone. He needs me.

Sania: Ok, I support you.

Mohit: Alisha has been your friend. Don't hide anything, and try to protect her. It will destroy Rahul's life.

Sania: I will share with Rahul everything I know once you reach the US.

Mohit: Alright, I'll begin the preparations. I have one more surprise for Rahul.

Mohit arrives in the United States and stays in the apartment provided by the company.

He visits and surprises Rahul.

Rahul: How come you are here?

Mohit: I'll talk about that later. What is the situation here?

Rahul: Finding a hostel for Vidya.

Mohit: Where is Alisha?

Rahul: Inside.

Mohit: And Vidya?

Rahul: At the University.

Alisha is unhappy about Mohit being in the US.

Alisha: What brings you here? Are you following me?

Mohit: I have been assigned a project.

Alisha: It doesn't seem that way. It feels like you might be keeping an eye on me. In any case, what would you like to have?

Mohit: Alisha's special.

Alisha: Ok.

Alisha goes to make some tea.

Rahul and Mohit start chatting, but as soon as Alisha brings the tea, they fall silent.

Alisha: Rahul, cooking is not my forte. After we get married, I plan to hire help.

Rahul: Let us see.

Alisha is taking a nap while Vidya returns from the university.

Mohit takes Rahul with him to his apartment.

They give a call to Sania

Mohit: Hi Sania, how are you?

Sania: I am good. How are you doing?

Mohit: I am doing well. Can you please speak to Rahul?

Sania: Yes.

Rahul: Hi. How are you, Sania?

Sania: I am doing good. I hope you are doing well.

Rahul: Somewhat yes.

Sania: I've noticed Alisha clinging to Vinay multiple times, and I'm uncertain about their relationship.

Maltesh works in the same organization, and I think he is aware of it. I'll check with him and let you know.

Rahul: Ok. Thank you for informing me.

Sania: Rahul, we truly want what is best for you.

Rahul: I am fortunate to have you guys in my life.

Sania: We too. Take care.

Mohit concludes the call with Sania by asking her to check with Maltesh.

Alisha and Vidya are at Rahul's Apartment.

Alisha: Did you find any place in the nearby hostel?

Vidya: No, I am still searching.

Alisha: Do it as soon as possible.

Vidya: I am trying to the best of my level.

Alisha: That's good.

In the meantime, Sania reaches out to Maltesh and requests him to investigate Alisha and Vinay's relationship.

Sania meets Maltesh in person.

Sania: I need evidence to prove Alisha is double-timing Vinay and Rahul. We can save Rahul.

Maltesh: Ok. I'll do it.

Maltesh skilfully investigates and identifies the perfect moment to engage with Vinay, and they confidently share a drink.

Vinay drinks excessively, allowing Maltesh an opportunityto check his phone. Maltesh asks for the password, which Vinay readily shares. Maltesh opens the phone and discovers pictures that prove Vinay and Alisha are having an affair.

Vinay shares the pictures with Sania. Sania thanks him.

Sania shares the pictures with Mohit.

Mohit and Rahul meet again

Mohit: Please take a look at these pictures to better understand what I was trying to convey earlier.

Rahul is devastated. The intense outrage sparked by the incident greatly impacts him.

Rahul: I devoted my life to Alisha, believing in our bond, but she chose to betray my trust.

Mohit: It's ok. You have a long life to go.

Meanwhile, Shashikala makes a call to Alisha.

Shashikala: How are you, Alisha?

Alisha: Fine, Mom. How are you all?

Shashikala: We all are fine. From now onwards, please focus on Rahul and get married to him as soon as possible.

Alisha: Yes, Mom. I am working on the same.

Shashikala: No more excuses this time. Strengthen your relationship. Where are you now?

Alisha: I am at his apartment, and Vidya has just returned from the university.

Shashikala: Ok. Shall I talk to her?

Alisha: Mom, why do you want to talk to her?

Shashikala: You don't understand. Give it to her.

Alisha hands over the phone, saying, "My mom wants to talk to you." Vidya wonders.

Shashikala: Hello beta, how are you doing?

Vidya: I am doing good. How about you?

Shashikala: I hope you are doing well. I have heard that your academic pursuits are progressing positively, and it is impressive to see how much you have grown. I appreciate your hard work and dedication.

Vidya: Thank you, aunty.

Shashikala: Despite all the bad things that happened to you, you stood against all odds. But Rahul has been your support system through your journey, right?

Vidya: Yes, aunty he is the one.

Shashikala: If you truly believe that, then you should definitely return his favor.

Vidya: Definitely. Anything for him.

Shashikala: I will explain how you can return the favour.

Vidya: Absolutely, aunty! Just let me know.

Shashikala: Please don't mind me saying this but you are becoming an obstacle between Rahul and Alisha.

Tears rolled down Vidya's cheeks.

They have been in a committed relationship for nine years, navigating the ups and downs together. However, in a difficult turn of events, he made the decision to marry you, motivated by a deep desire to protect and support you during a challenging time. Don't you want him to be happy?

Vidya: Yes, I want him to be happy.

Shashikala: Find a nearby hostel or place and leave his location. If you require any financial assistance, I am willing to help.

In the future, I will help you find a husband as well.

Please try to understand and appreciate the depth of a mother's heart.

Vidya: I understand the situation and will leave the place as soon as possible.

Vidya hands over the phone to Alisha and immediately rushes to her bedroom. She cries in deep.

Alisha talks to her mother

Alisha: What did you tell her mom?

Shashikala: I have spoken to her, and I now believe she will not hinder your relationship. I will call you later.

Vidya calls some of her friends to ask if she can stay with them in their hostel, but they inform her that there is no vacancy.

She remembers Jessica and calls her. During the call, she cries and asks if Jessica has a place for her to stay. Jessica instantly responds that Vidya can stay with her for as long as she needs. Jessica comes and picks Vidya.

Jessica (at Rahul's residence): Jessica (Ringing the bell, and Alisha opens the door): Hi, This is Jessica, Rahul's friend. You are Alisha, right?

Alisha: Ya.

Jessica: Where is Rahul?

Alisha: He is outside, working on something. Rahul had girlfriends in the US as well. (taunting Jessica)

Jessica: Hey, hold on. We are just friends. Yes, I proposed to him, but he rejected my proposal. Now, I am committed to Manish.

Alisha: I don't believe you, girls. You could have been double-timing.

Jessica: Please take a moment to consider your words. It seems you might be sharing thoughts without much reflection.

Anyway, I have come to pick up Vidya. Where is she?

Alisha: She is inside.

Jessica goes and asks if anything is wrong. Vidya cries and Jessica packs her bag.

Jessica: Vidya, shall we go home and talk?

Vidya shakes her head in agreement.

As Jessica and Vidya are leaving…

Alisha: Finally, you are leaving the place. My mother's strategy worked. Do you want something to eat before leaving?

Jessica: Shut your mouth.

Alisha: Vidya, before leaving sign these divorce papers.

Vidya signs and goes.

Alisha tells her mother that half of the work has been completed.

At Jessica's house, Vidya shares everything that happened, including how Alisha and her mother asked her to leave.

Jessica: Look, God is watching everything. But why did you sign the papers? I mean….

Vidya: They have been in a relationship for nine years. I am not inclined to interfere in their relationship, as he has been very supportive of me during this time.

Jessica: I understand completely, but I don't think he is happy with her.

Vidya: I don't understand.

Jessica: You don't take stress. Suppose there is some connection between you. It will come back.

Vidya gets a call from her friend Amaira.

Amaira: Hey Vidya, are you not going to participate in the dance competition?

Vidya: No.

Amaira: You have prepared well for this, dear. So, what seems to be the problem?

Vidya: The person who inspired me to dance will no longer be in my life.

Amaira: What?

Vidya: I don't have anything to share right now. I'll call you later.

Amaira: Okay, but please take a moment to consider it.

Vidya: Ya sure.

Suddenly, Jessica snatches Vidya's phone and asks Amaira about the issue. Amaira replies that Vidya doesn't want to participate in the dance competition, even though she prepared well for it.

Jessica: Why are you not participating in the dance competition?

Vidya: Rahul motivated me to dance, but he won't be a part of my life anymore.

Jessica: Some time ago, I also proposed to him, but he rejected me. Is he not a part of my life? Please do it.

Vidya: Ok.

Jessica informs Rahul about the competition and encourages him to attend, and Rahul agrees.

On the day of the competition-

Jessica prepares Vidya and waits for Rahul.

Rahul and Mohit arrive at the dance hall together.

While Vidya dances.

Rahul: I can relate to this in some way. I don't understand.

Mohit: Do you remember when you lost to Mahaveer International School?

Rahul: Yes, we were in the eleventh grade.

Mohit: And you liked a girl's dance.

Rahul: Yes. I can relate it to the same dance.

Mohit smiles, and after the performance, Vidya wins second place in the competition.

They congratulate Vidya and ask Jessica to take care of her.

Rahul: Jessi, we are going to India to execute something. Please take care of Vidya until we return.

Jessica: But why did it happen so suddenly?

Rahul: Everything will fall into place. Vidya. Take care while we're in India. We'll return soon.

Rahul, Mohit, and Alisha are going to India.

In the flight-

Alisha: I always knew you would come back for me.

Rahul: Yes.

After arriving in India, they take a moment to rest before heading to Alisha's house.

In Alisha's house-

Shashikala and Shailesh welcome everyone.

Shashikala: Rahul, I knew that your love is true.

Rahul: Yes, my love is true madam.

Alisha: Please sign the divorce papers so we can get married.

Rahul: I will do that, but before signing the papers, I would like to show you something.

Rahul shows all the photos of Vinay and Alisha on the projector.

Shailesh was taken aback, but Shashikala was already aware of the situation.

Alisha: I didn't do it intentionally; it was just a brief affair. You also had friends in the US, and I'm unsure of the relationships you had there. You've been with Vidya for a year and a half now. How can I trust you?

Rahul: I don't have any expectations from the people like you.

Shashikala: Please forgive her, Rahul. I know it is not a small mistake. She is immature, and you are well aware of it.

Rahul: Madam, it was not a mistake that she betrayed me. I devoted myself to you completely and never turned my attention to anyone else. For the past nine years, I have been loyal to you. However, please don't expect me to maintain that loyalty any longer.

I can't divorce Vidya; I love her and want to be with her for the rest of my life.

Sorry, Alisha.

Alisha apologizes to him repeatedly, but he doesn't listen to her.

Shailesh and Shashikala are silent; they feel ashamed of their daughter.

Rahul: I didn't expect this from you, Shashi madam. You were my favorite lecturer. You expelled Vidya from my apartment and didn't inform me about Vinay and Alisha's affair.

Mohit: Please allow him to be happy now. It is my humble request to all of you.

After meeting his parents, Rahul convinces them about his marriage to Vidya, and then he and Mohit fly back to the US.

On the way to the US.

Mohit: Rahul, do you know why you felt a connection to the fest in 11th grade during Vidya's performance?

Rahul: Why?

Mohit: Vidya is the same girl you liked and dreamed about, reminding you that your heart knows what it truly desires.

Rahul (Astonished): How did you know that?

Mohit: In August, when I spent time with you all in the US, I casually asked Vidya about her education. She mentioned that she studied at Mahaveer International School.

Later, when we started discussing dance, she shared that she learned the Kathak form, although her dad was against it. Also, she is four years younger than us. Considering all these points, I inquired with her parents, and her mother showed me an old picture from that fest. Do you recognize her?

Rahul recognizes her and his heart is overwhelmed with joy.

Mohit: You scolded me many times because of her. I still remember that we went to the school to find out who she was before Alisha came into your life. You were crazy about her.

Rahul smiles as he gazes at the picture, savoring the powerful memories it evokes.

Rahul gives Vidya a surprise.

Rahul: Vidya, I love you and want to be with you forever. Do you see me as your husband?

Tears of joy streamed down her cheeks.

She accepted his love, and Jessica, Manish, Vipul, and Mohit joined in celebrating it.

Here, Alisha becomes mentally unstable as Vinay starts ignoring her.

She is admitted to the mental hospital for treatment.

For some days she doesn't respond to any treatment. Her parents become worried.

Maltesh feels pity for her and becomes her support system during the treatment. He somewhere feels he shouldn't have exposed her.

She eventually begins to respond to the treatment and feels comfortable with Maltesh. She cries in front of him, acknowledging her mistakes and promising to change in the future.

Maltesh: Let go of the past, and I apologize for putting you in that position.

Alisha: It was my mistake; you don't need to apologize.

Maltesh: I feel a strong connection with you. Will you be my better half?

www.ingramcontent.com/pod-product-compliance
Lightning Source LLC
LaVergne TN
LVHW061556070526
838199LV00077B/7073